Using Science to Make Art

John Burdess and Jonathon Phillips
Photographs by Lindsay Edwards

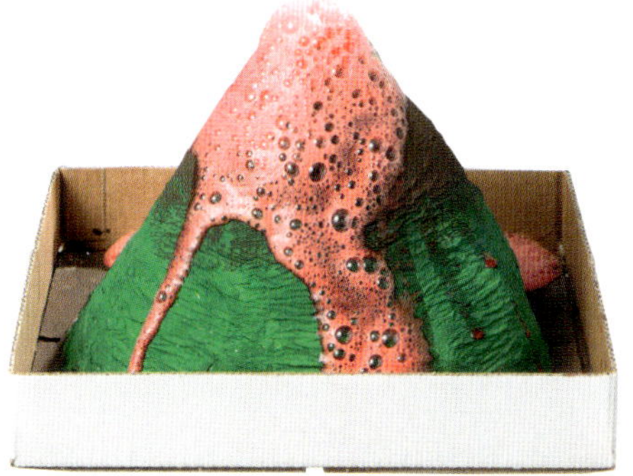

Contents

Science and Art

> *Science and art sometimes can touch one another, like two pieces of the jigsaw puzzle which is our human life …*
>
> – M. C. Escher (artist)

Artists are known for their creativity, or their ability to use their imaginations to invent and make things. However, scientists need to be creative, too. Artists use their creative skills to make wonderful works of art, and scientists use their creative skills to solve problems. Art can also help us to understand and enjoy scientific processes.

In this book, there are two activities that use science to make colourful and exciting artworks.

This art using living microbes is so small it can only be seen through a microscope.

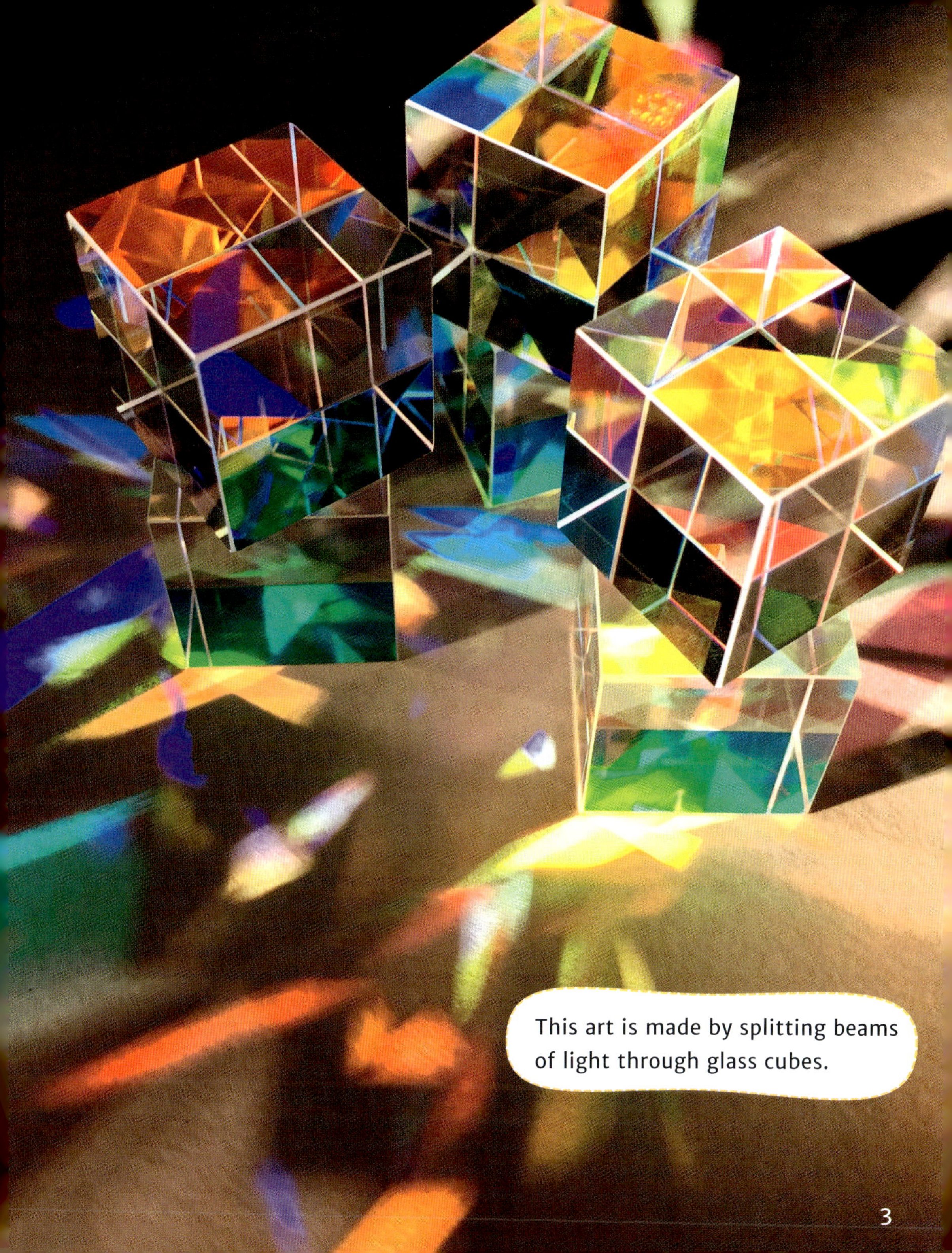

This art is made by splitting beams of light through glass cubes.

Make a Model of an Erupting Volcano

How a Volcano Erupts

A volcano is a mountain or hill with an opening in its surface. A volcanic eruption occurs when hot gases and melted rock, called **magma**, move up to Earth's surface through cracks. Some flows across the land as **lava**; some explodes into the air as volcanic ash. This is similar to when a can of fizzy drink is shaken up. Pressure builds up inside the can. When the can is opened, the pressure is released and the liquid sprays out.

When a volcano erupts it can cause widespread destruction. But it can also create fertile soil for farming, and new landforms.

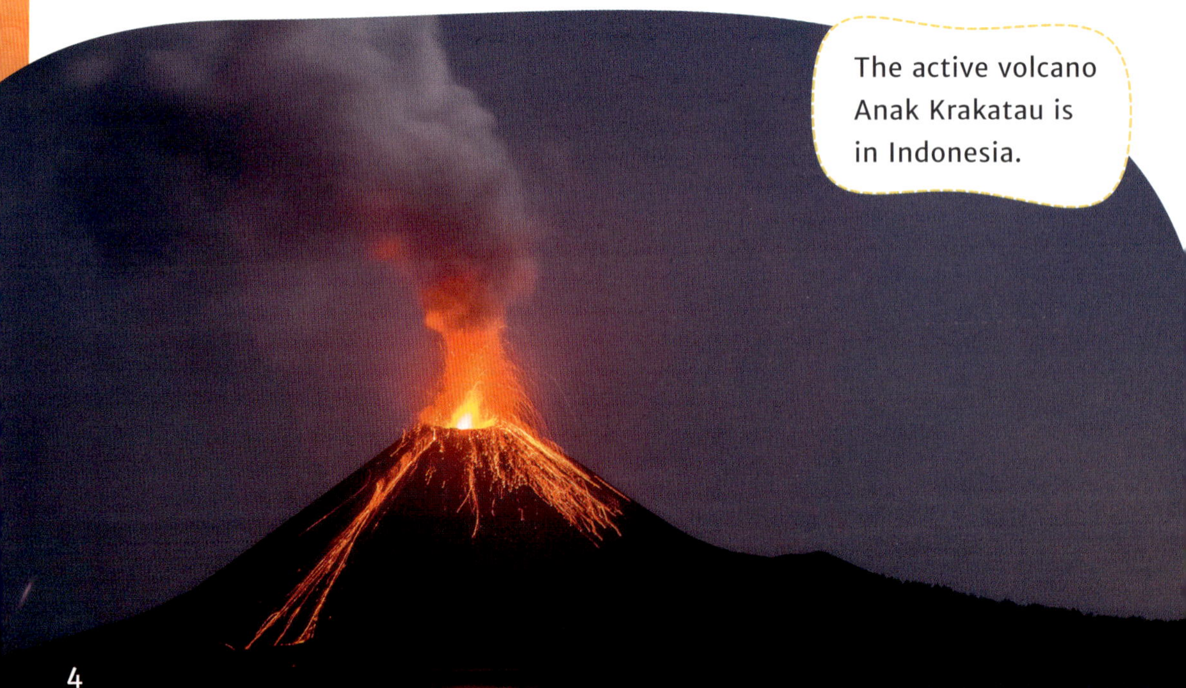

The active volcano Anak Krakatau is in Indonesia.

Goal

To make a model showing what happens when a volcano erupts

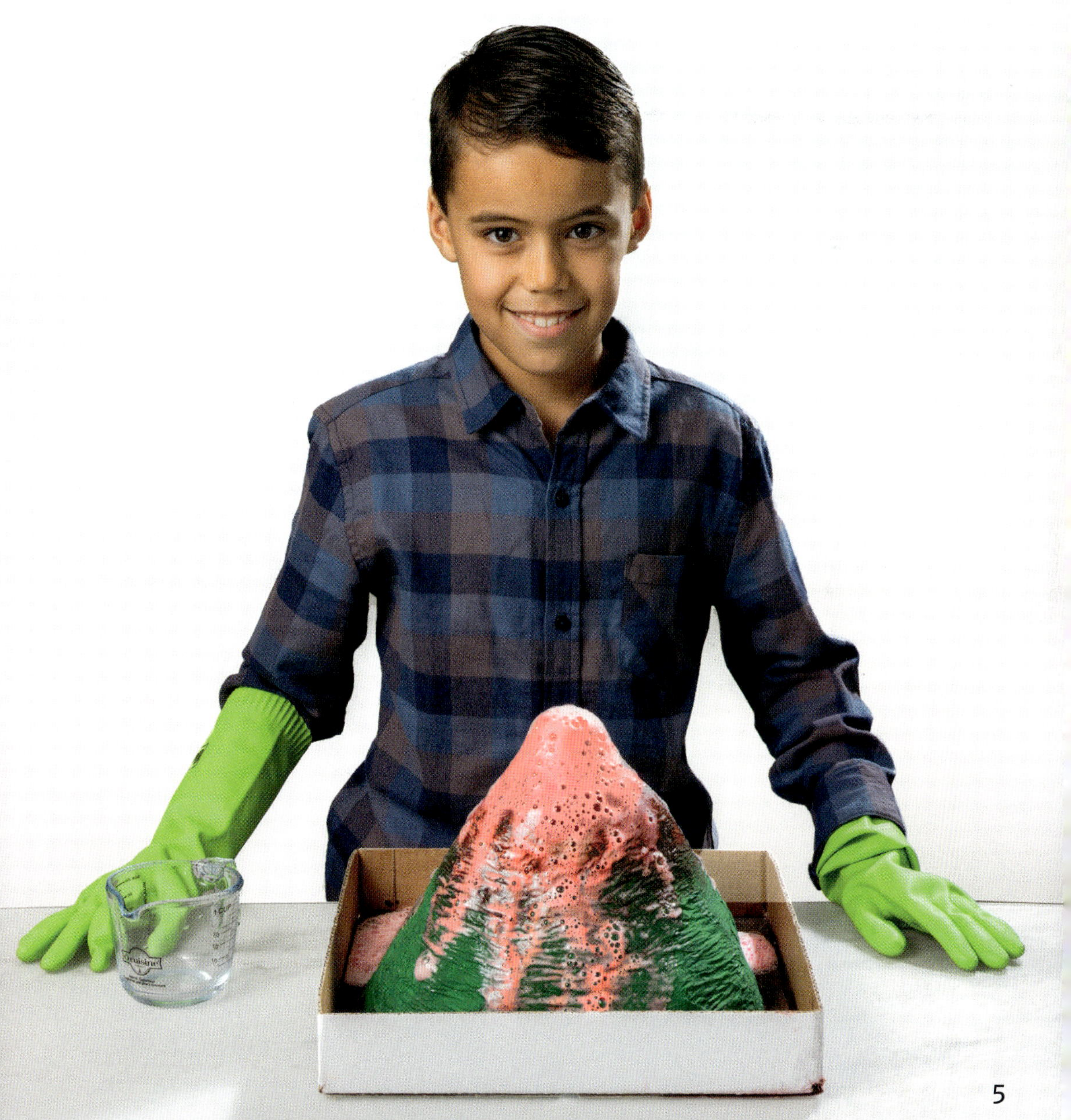

Materials

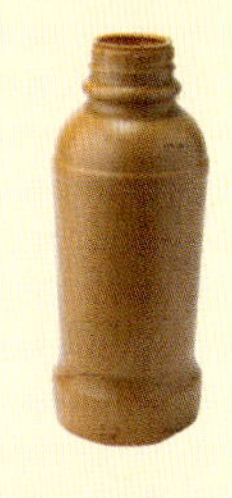

- a clean, empty plastic bottle (lid removed), about 16 centimetres tall

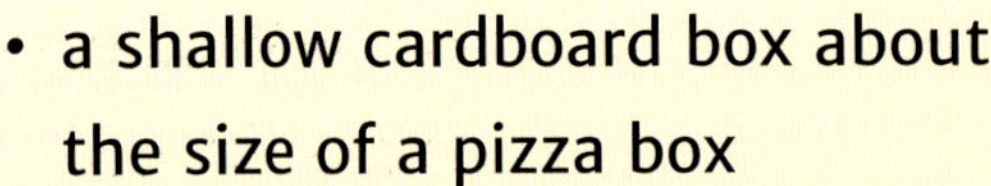

- a shallow cardboard box about the size of a pizza box

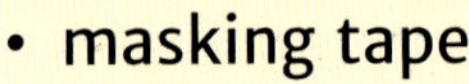

- masking tape

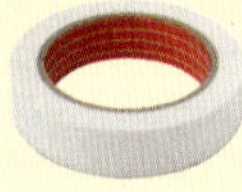

- 20 sheets of newspaper
- some plastic containers

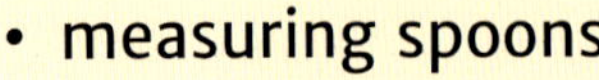

- measuring spoons

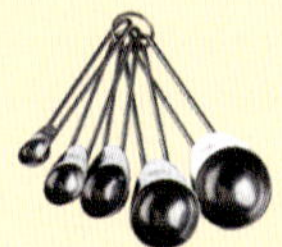

- white glue

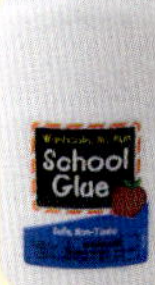

- a box of tissues

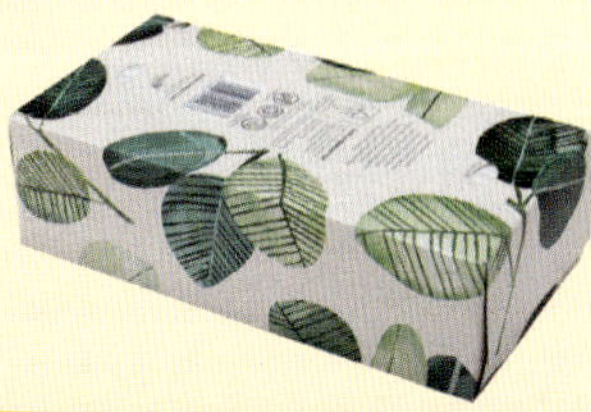

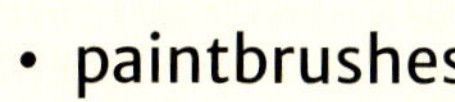

- paintbrushes

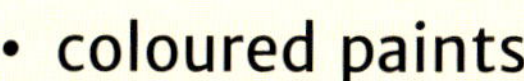

- coloured paints

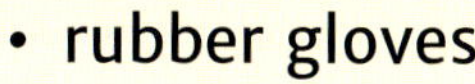

- rubber gloves

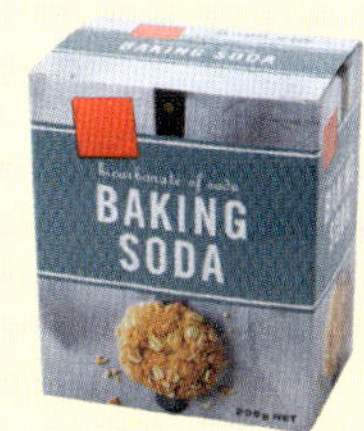

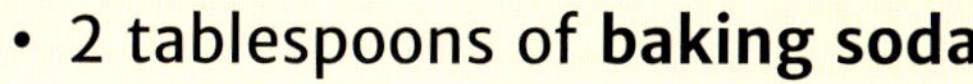

- 2 tablespoons of **baking soda**

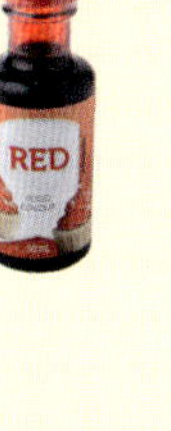

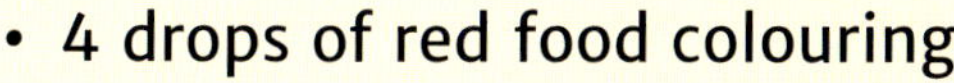

- 4 drops of red food colouring

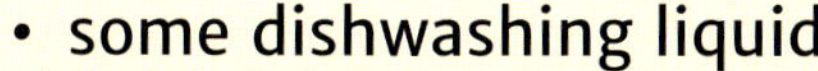

- some dishwashing liquid

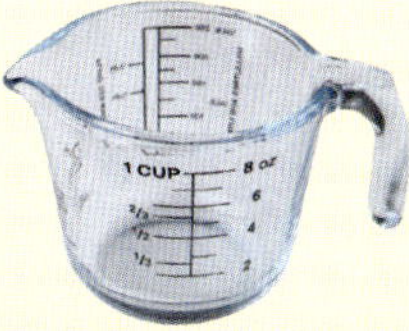

- a small jug
- 8 tablespoons of white vinegar

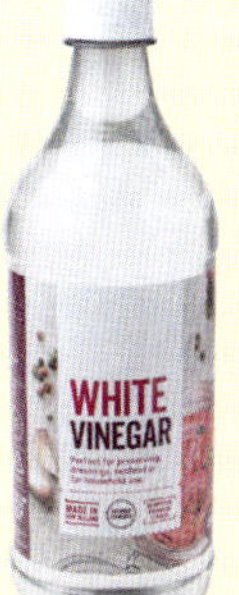

- a funnel

Steps

Build the Volcano

1. Stand the plastic bottle upright in the centre of the cardboard box. Use masking tape to fix it in place.

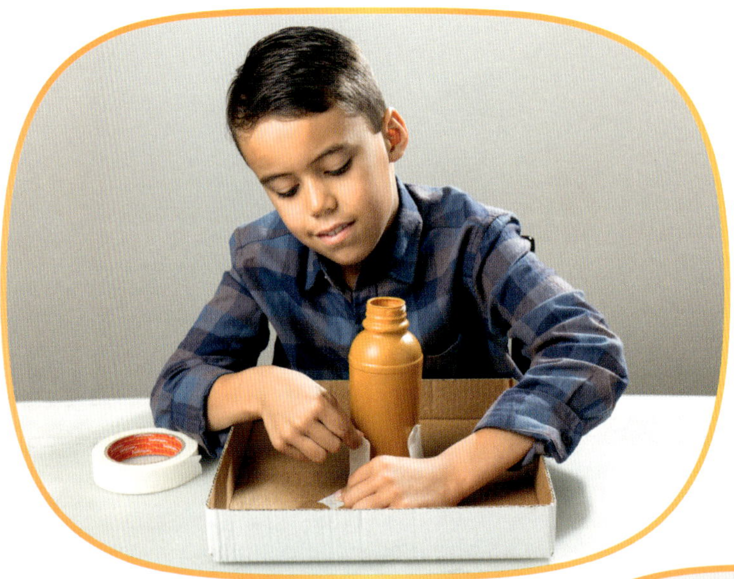

2. Screw up the sheets of newspaper into tight balls. Place the balls in layers on top of each other, until they reach the top of the bottle. (Make sure the newspaper does not cover the opening of the bottle.)

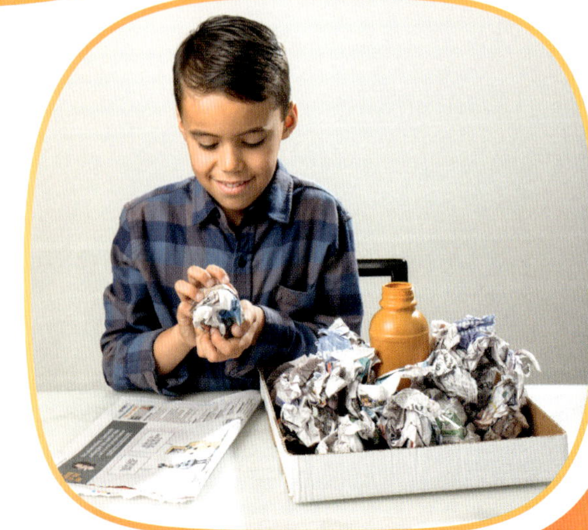

3. Squeeze and press the pile of newspaper to form a cone shape, like a volcano.

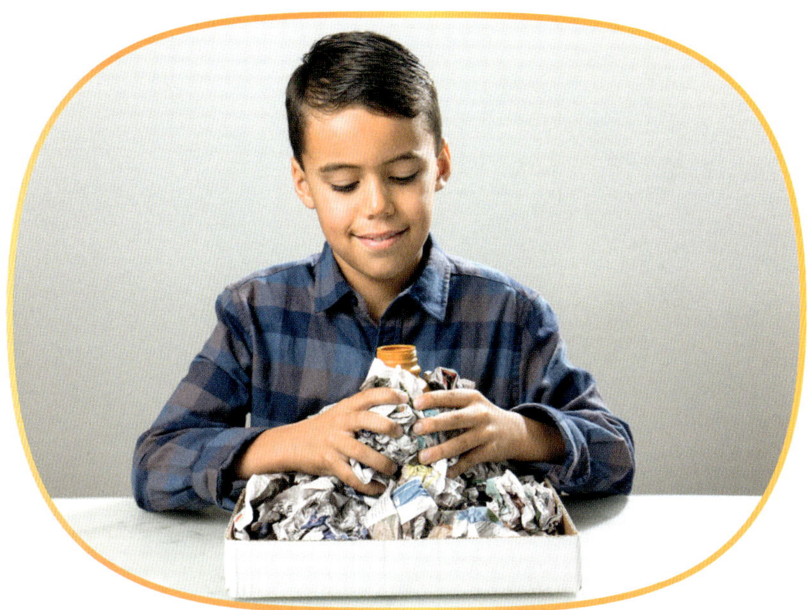

4. Put some long pieces of masking tape from top to bottom on the volcano. This will hold the newspaper in place.

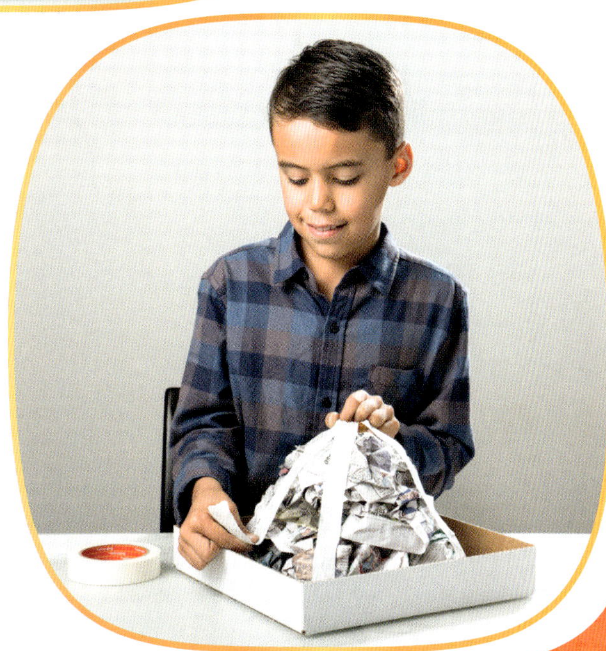

5. In one of the plastic containers, mix a tablespoon of glue with two tablespoons of water.

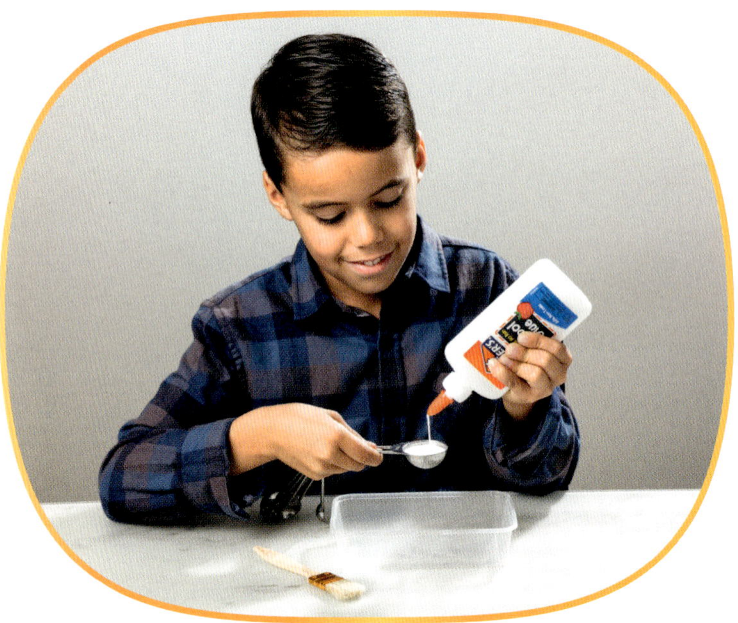

6. Carefully place a layer of tissues onto the volcano. You will need about 50 tissues to cover the volcano.

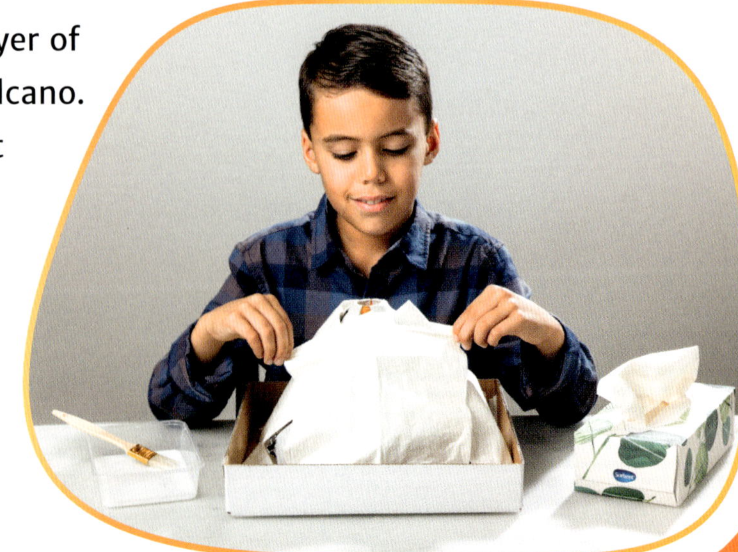

7. Next, gently brush the glue-and-water mixture over the tissues. Make sure the whole volcano is covered in tissues and glue, except the bottle opening at the top. The glue will soak through the tissues so they stick to the volcano.

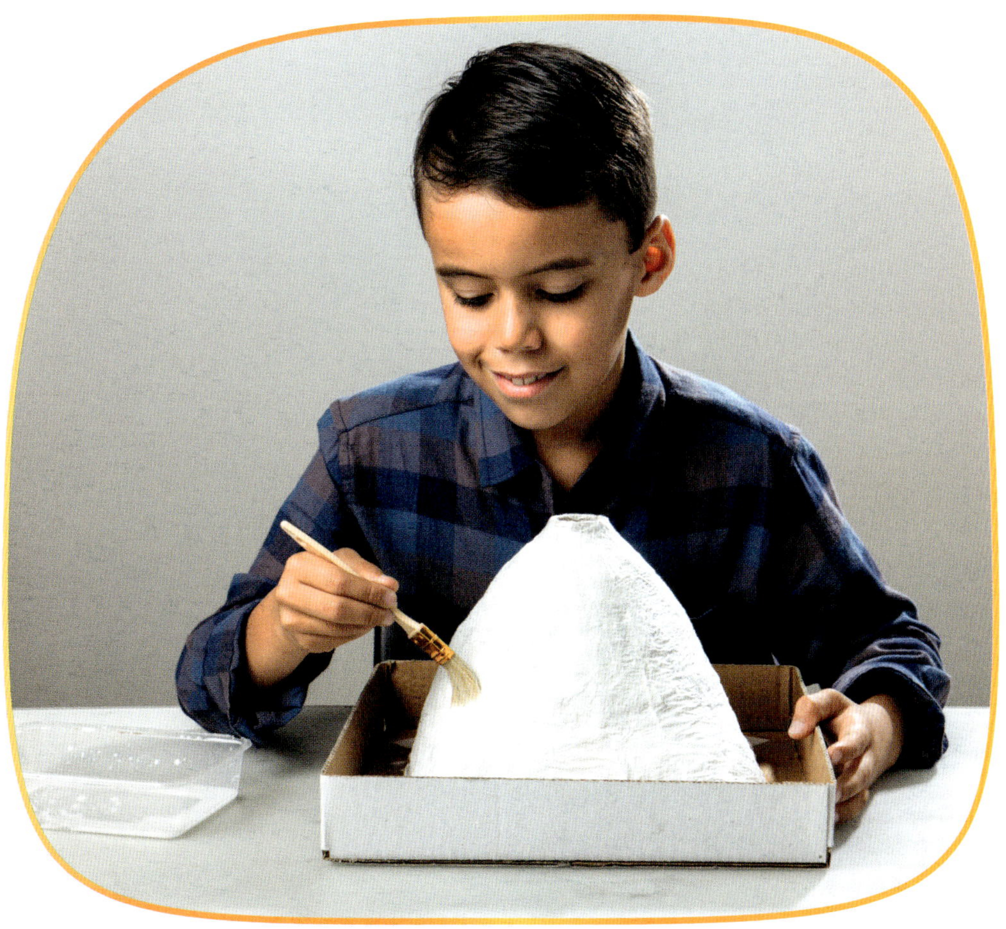

8. Leave the volcano overnight to dry.

Paint the Volcano

1. Mix some paints together in plastic containers to make the colours you would like your volcano to be.

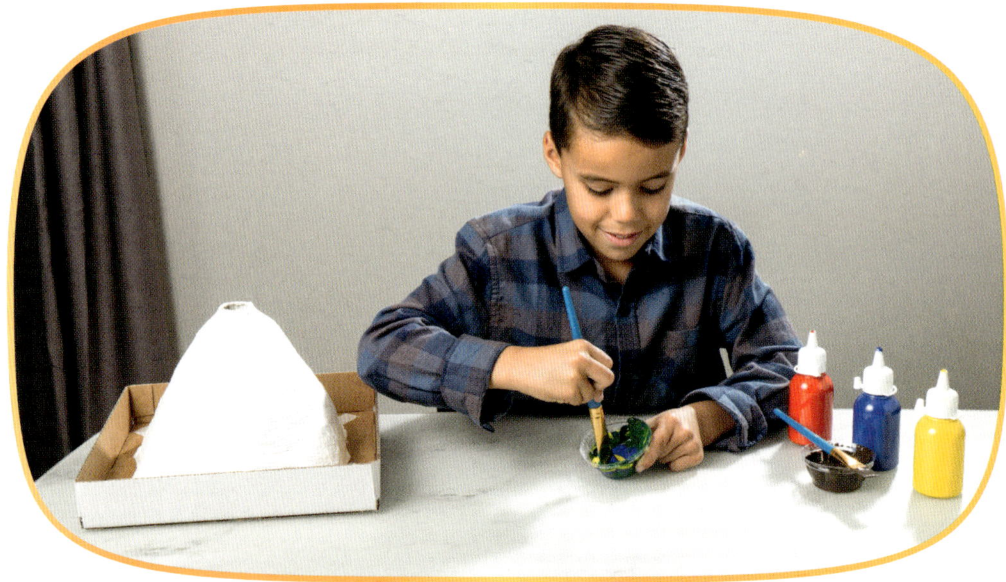

2. Paint all over your volcano. To avoid unpainted white spots, **dab** with your brush so the bristles reach into the small gaps.

3. Leave the paint to dry for at least four hours.

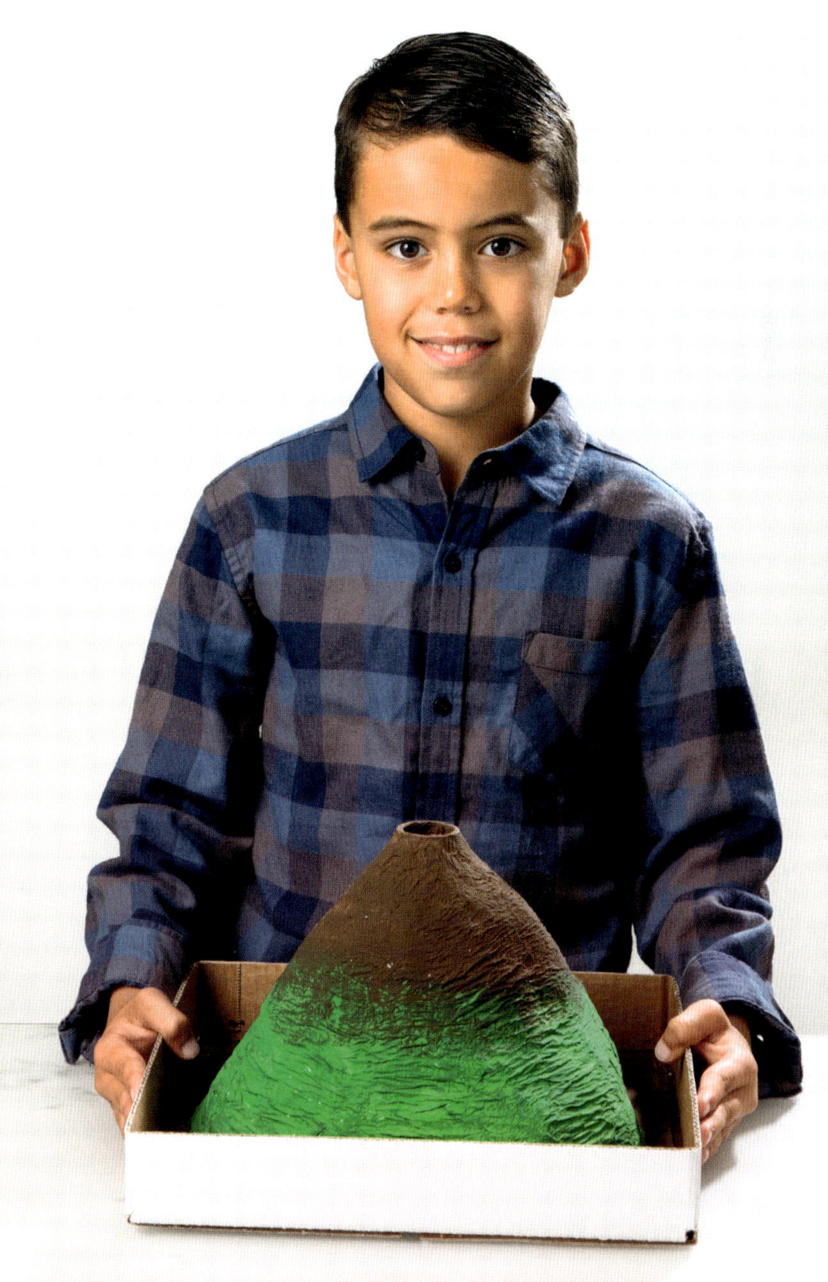

Make the Volcano Erupt

1. Put on the rubber gloves.
2. Put four drops of red food colouring, two tablespoons of baking soda and a squirt of dishwashing liquid into the bottle opening at the top of the volcano.

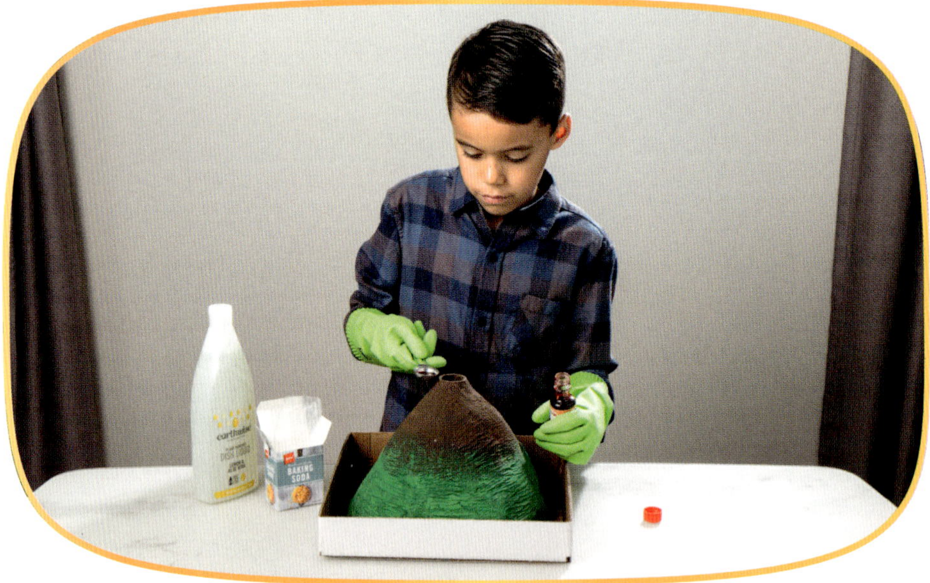

3. Next, measure out eight tablespoons of vinegar into the jug.

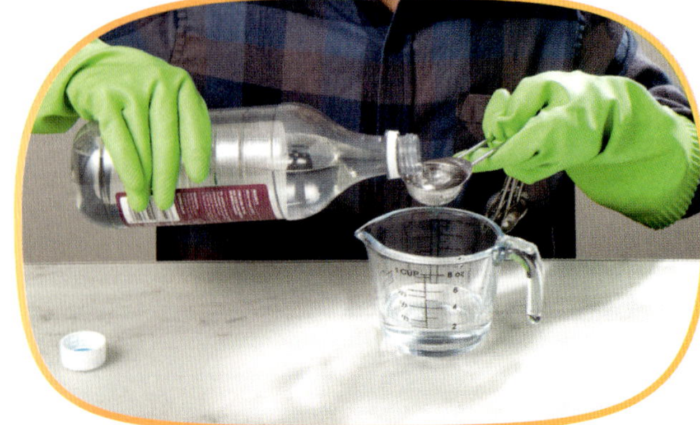

4. Place the funnel in the bottle opening. Then, ask an adult to help you carefully pour the vinegar from the jug into the top of the volcano.

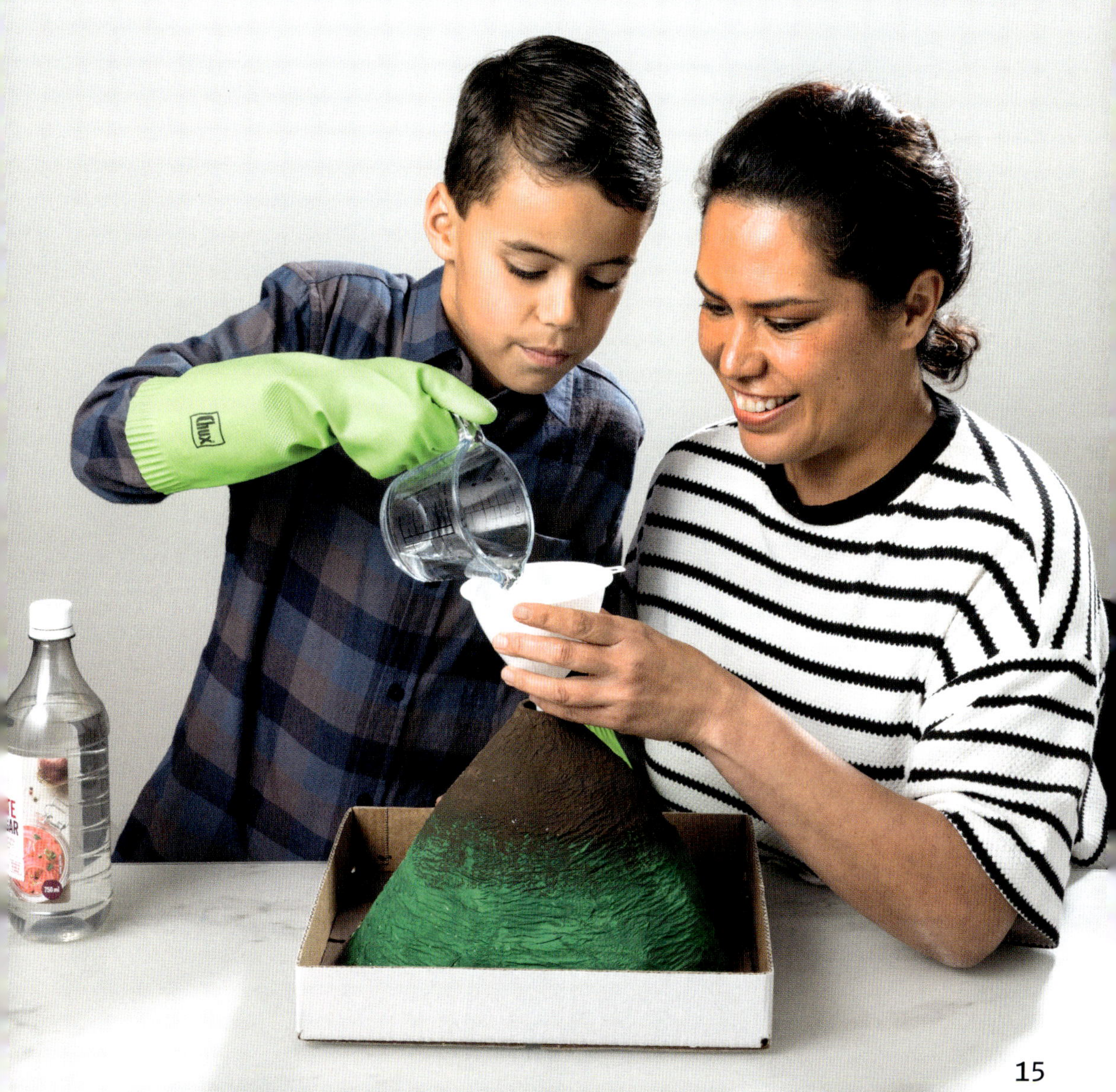

5. Watch what happens. The red food dye mixture will fizz and bubble out of the top of the volcano and run down the sides, just like magma!

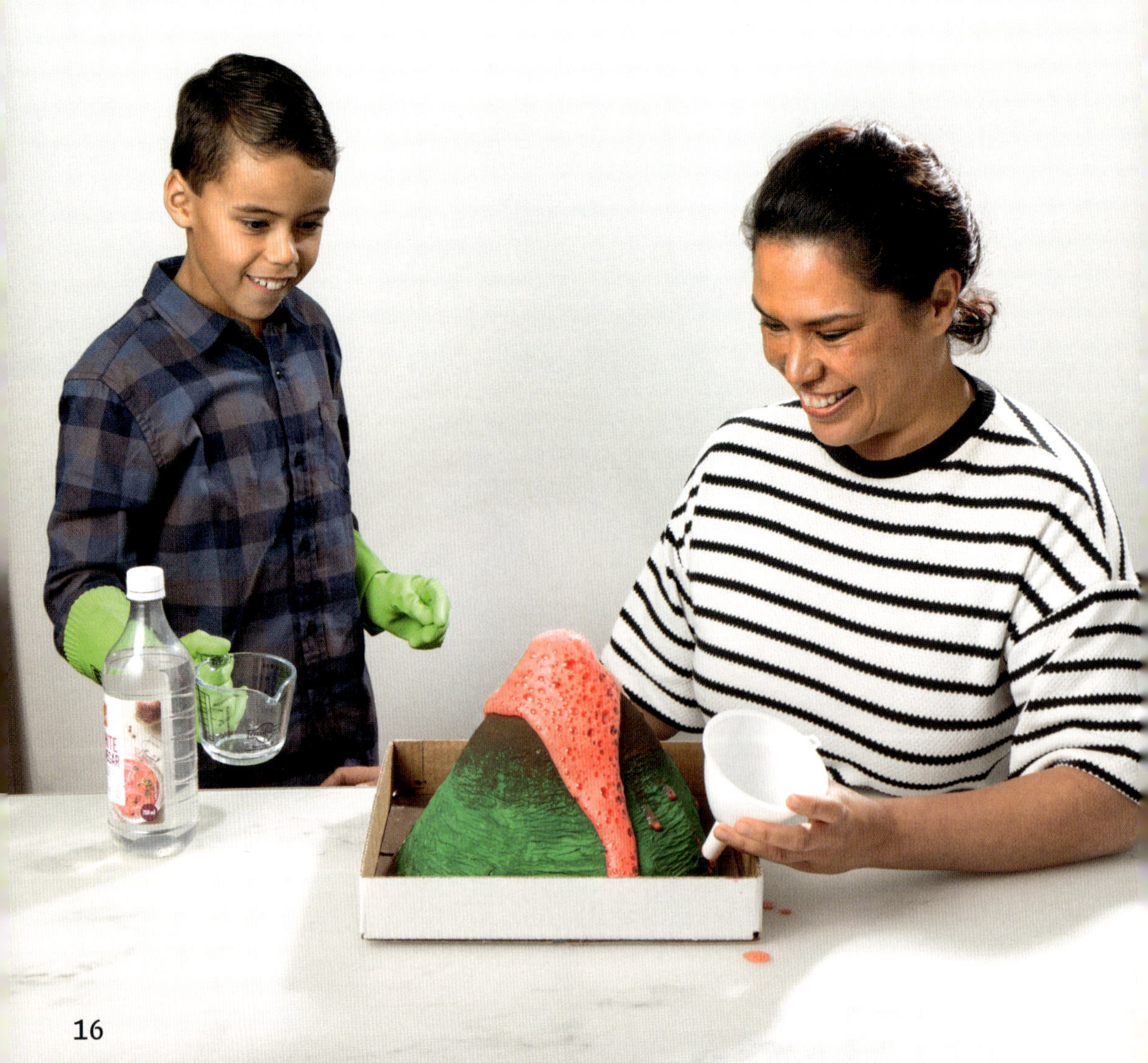

Explaining the Science

When vinegar and baking soda are mixed together, they react to make a gas called **carbon dioxide**. The gas builds up inside the bottle until it forces its way out of the top. The dishwashing liquid traps the bubbles created by the eruption. That makes the eruption last longer.

Deep under the ground, magma can do the same thing. It will rise up to Earth's surface and burst out of the volcano as lava!

Inside the Model Volcano

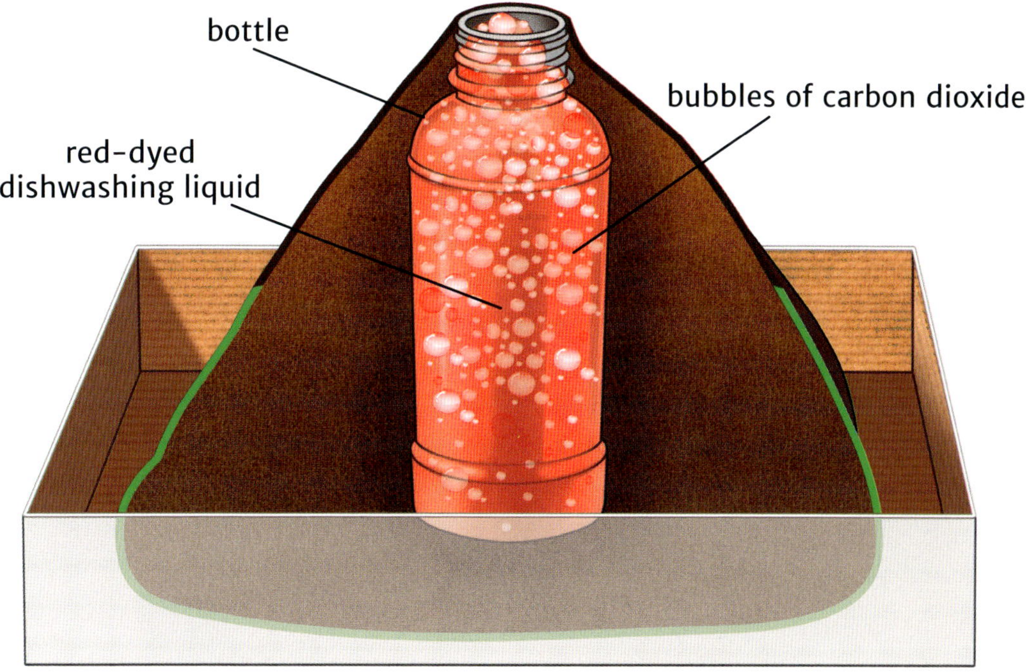

The carbon dioxide bubbles rise until the "lava" mixture erupts from the top of the bottle.

Make a Rube Goldberg Machine

What Is a Rube Goldberg Machine?

Rube Goldberg was an American cartoonist and **engineer** in the early to mid-twentieth century who was famous for his drawings of imaginary machines. His machines solved simple problems in complicated ways, using everyday materials. A Rube Goldberg machine might be designed to do a common action such as opening a door, using things like a **lever**, a **wheel and axle**, or even animals like mice!

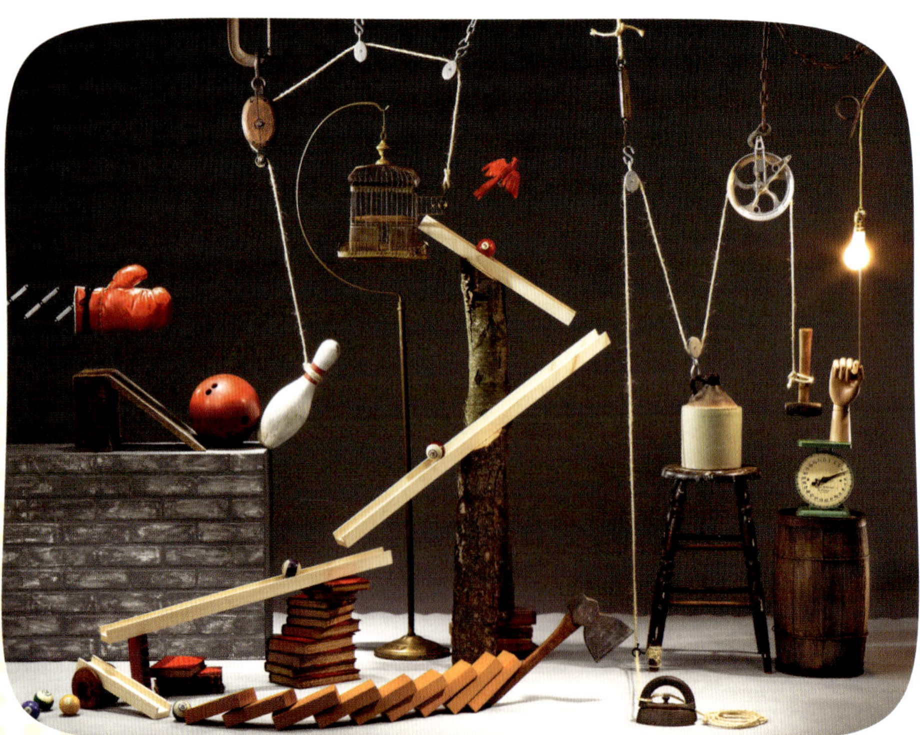

This Rube Goldberg machine turns on a light bulb.

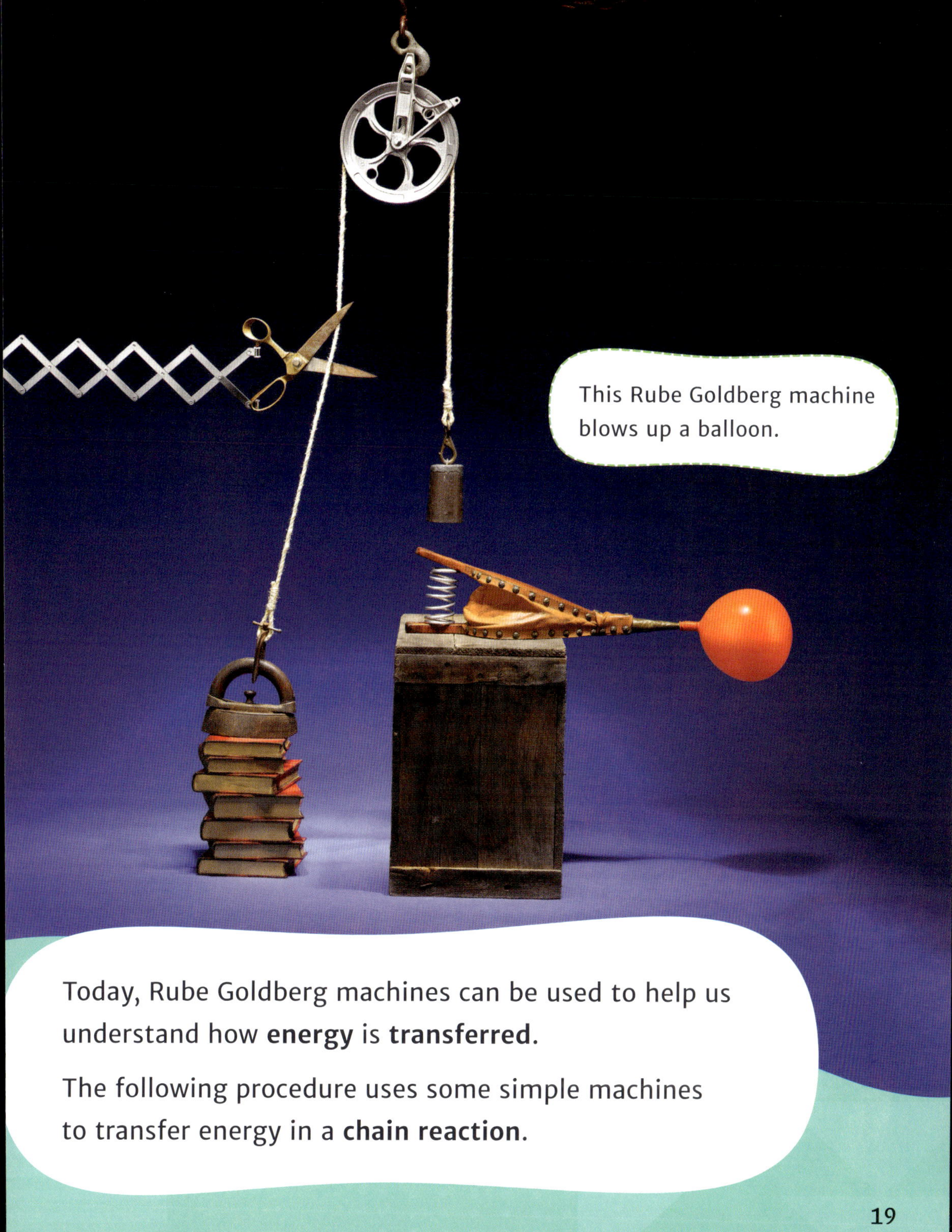

Today, Rube Goldberg machines can be used to help us understand how **energy** is **transferred**.

The following procedure uses some simple machines to transfer energy in a **chain reaction**.

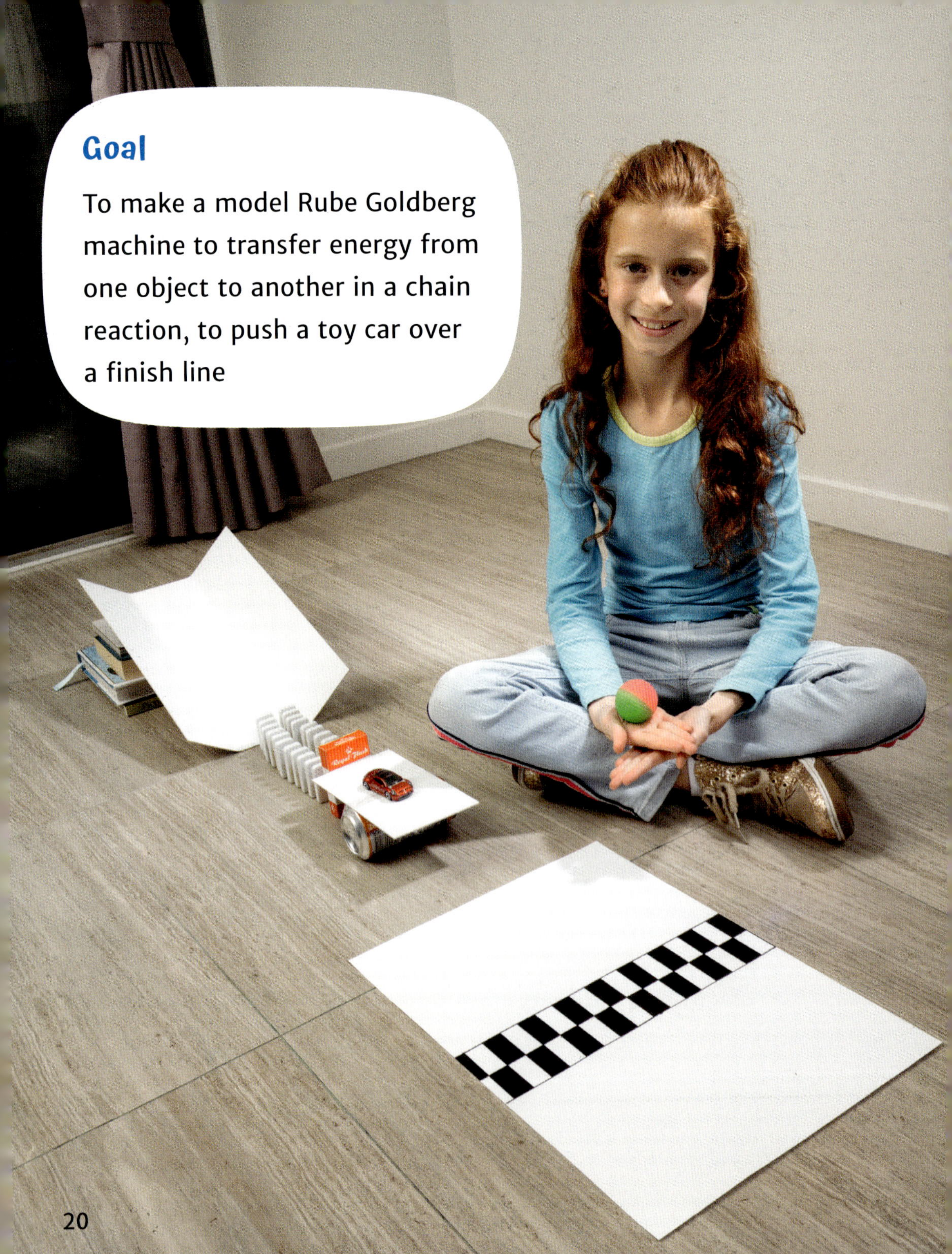

Goal

To make a model Rube Goldberg machine to transfer energy from one object to another in a chain reaction, to push a toy car over a finish line

Materials

- an A3 piece of cardboard
- a stack of books, at least 10 centimetres high

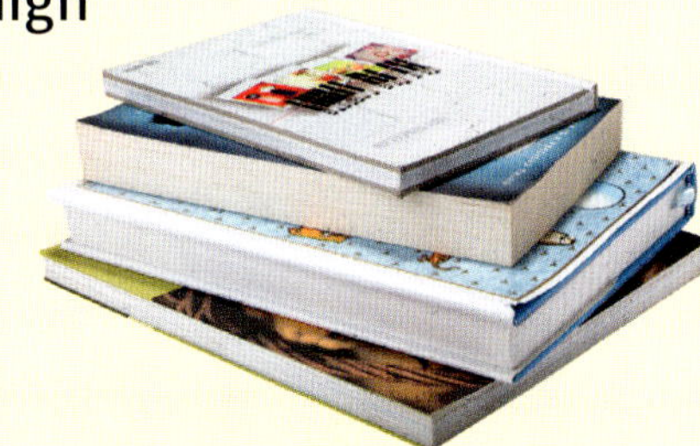

- 22 dominoes

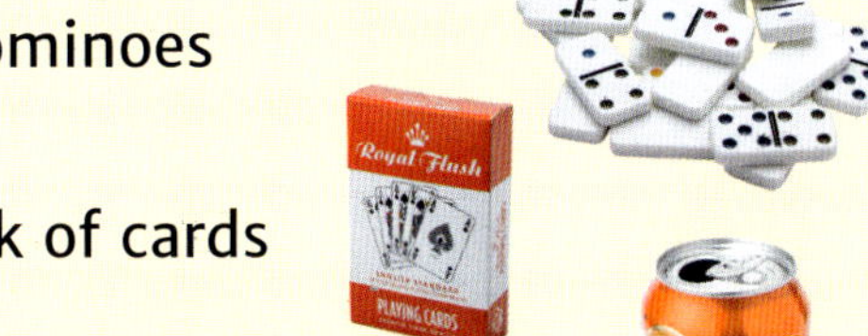

- a pack of cards

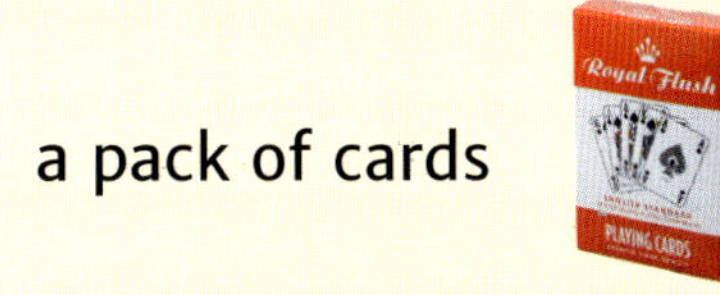

- a clean empty drink can
- an A5 piece of cardboard
- scissors

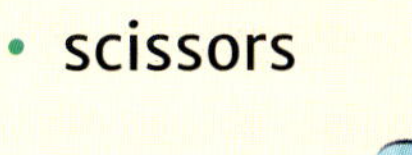

- tape

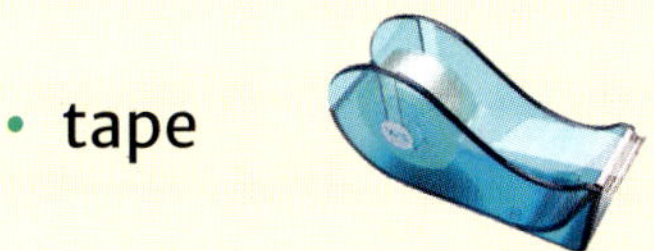

- a toy car
- a black marker

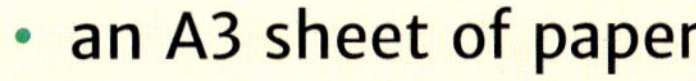

- an A3 sheet of paper
- a small ball

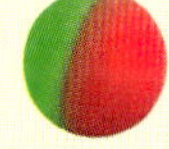

- a ruler

Steps

Set Up the Machine

1. Take the larger piece of cardboard and fold the long edges towards the middle to create two creases. Unfold the cardboard again.

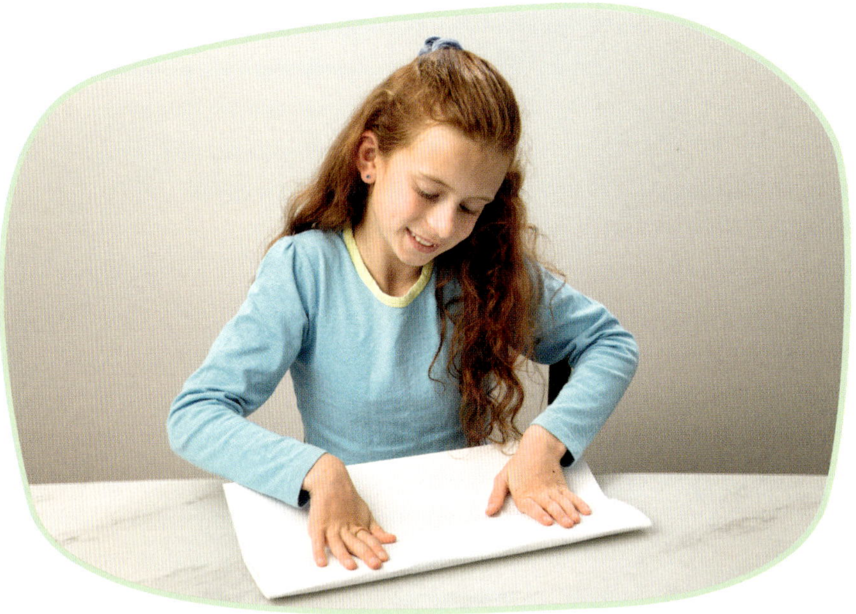

2. Find a clear, flat area on the floor. Stack the books in a pile on the floor. Then, lean the cardboard against the pile of books to make a **ramp**. This will be the first step in your chain reaction.

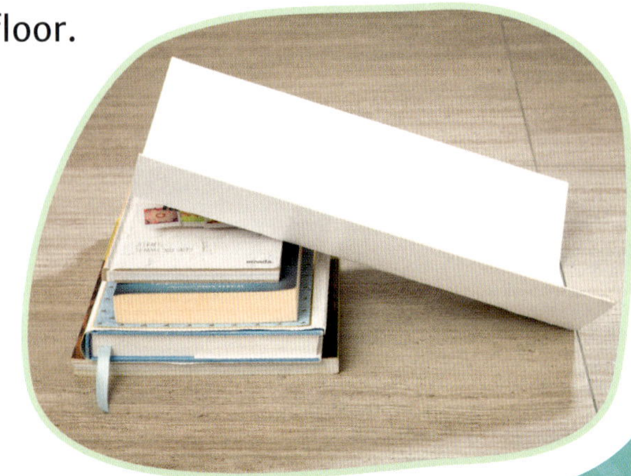

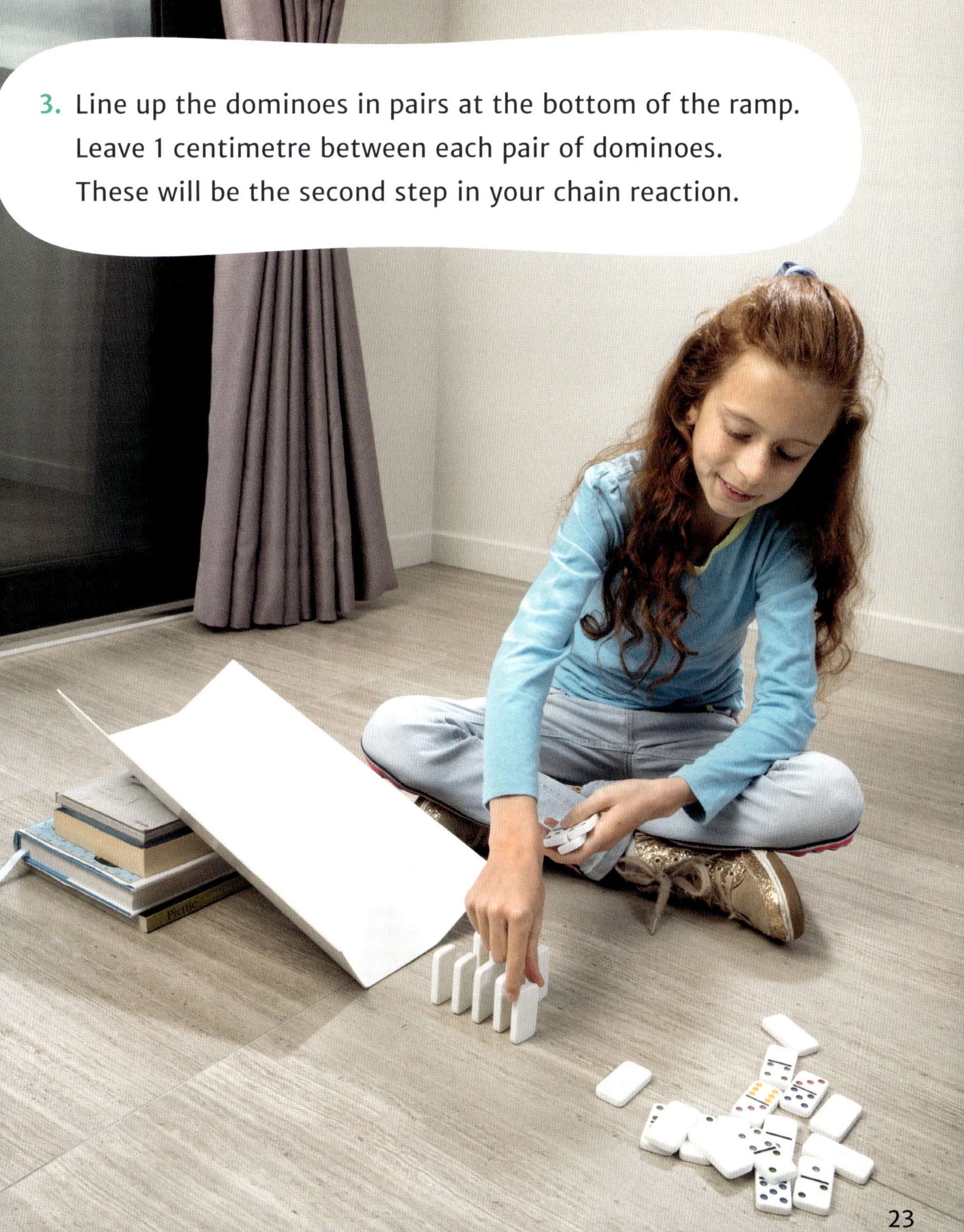

3. Line up the dominoes in pairs at the bottom of the ramp. Leave 1 centimetre between each pair of dominoes. These will be the second step in your chain reaction.

4. Take the pack of cards and stand it upright at the opposite end of the dominoes from the ramp. Position the pack within one domino's length of the last domino pair. The dominoes will strike the pack of cards as they fall. This will be the third step in your chain reaction.

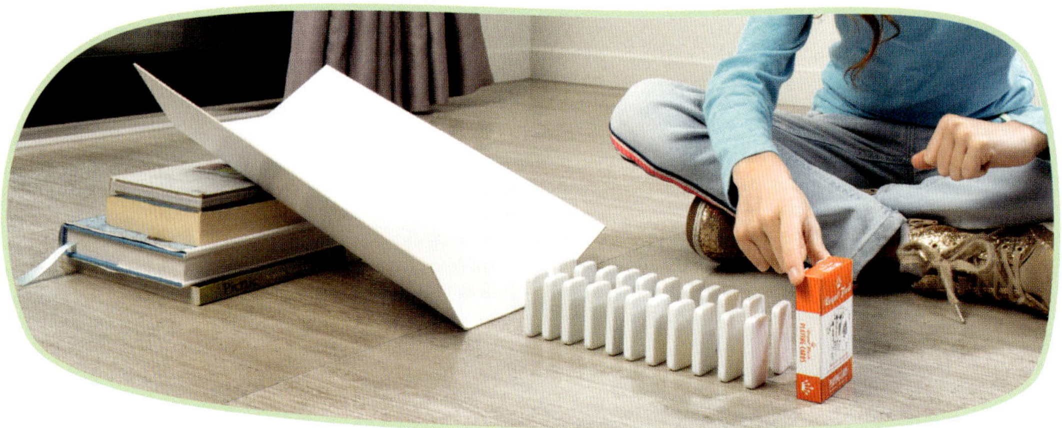

5. Cut off part of the smaller piece of cardboard along the long edge, so that the cardboard is the same width as the drink can.

6. Tape the empty can to the middle of the piece of cardboard. This will be the lever in your chain reaction. Place it after the pack of cards, so that the end of the cardboard is resting gently against the pack of cards.

7. Balance the toy car on top of the cardboard lever, facing away from the pack of cards. The toy car is the wheel and axle in your chain reaction.

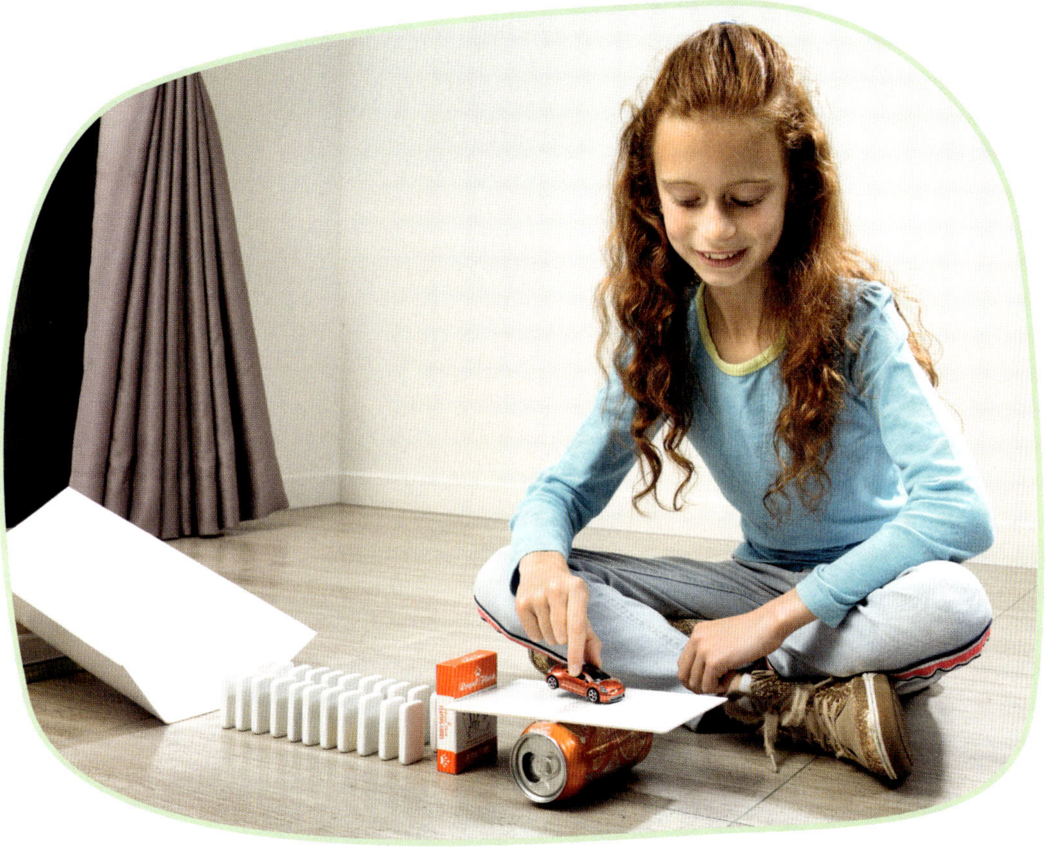

8. Draw a finish line on the sheet of paper using the black marker and the ruler. Place the sheet of paper at the opposite side of the car to the pack of cards.

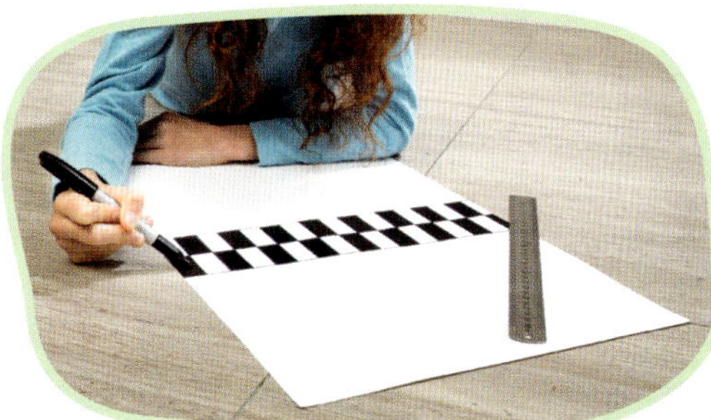

Your Rube Goldberg machine is ready!

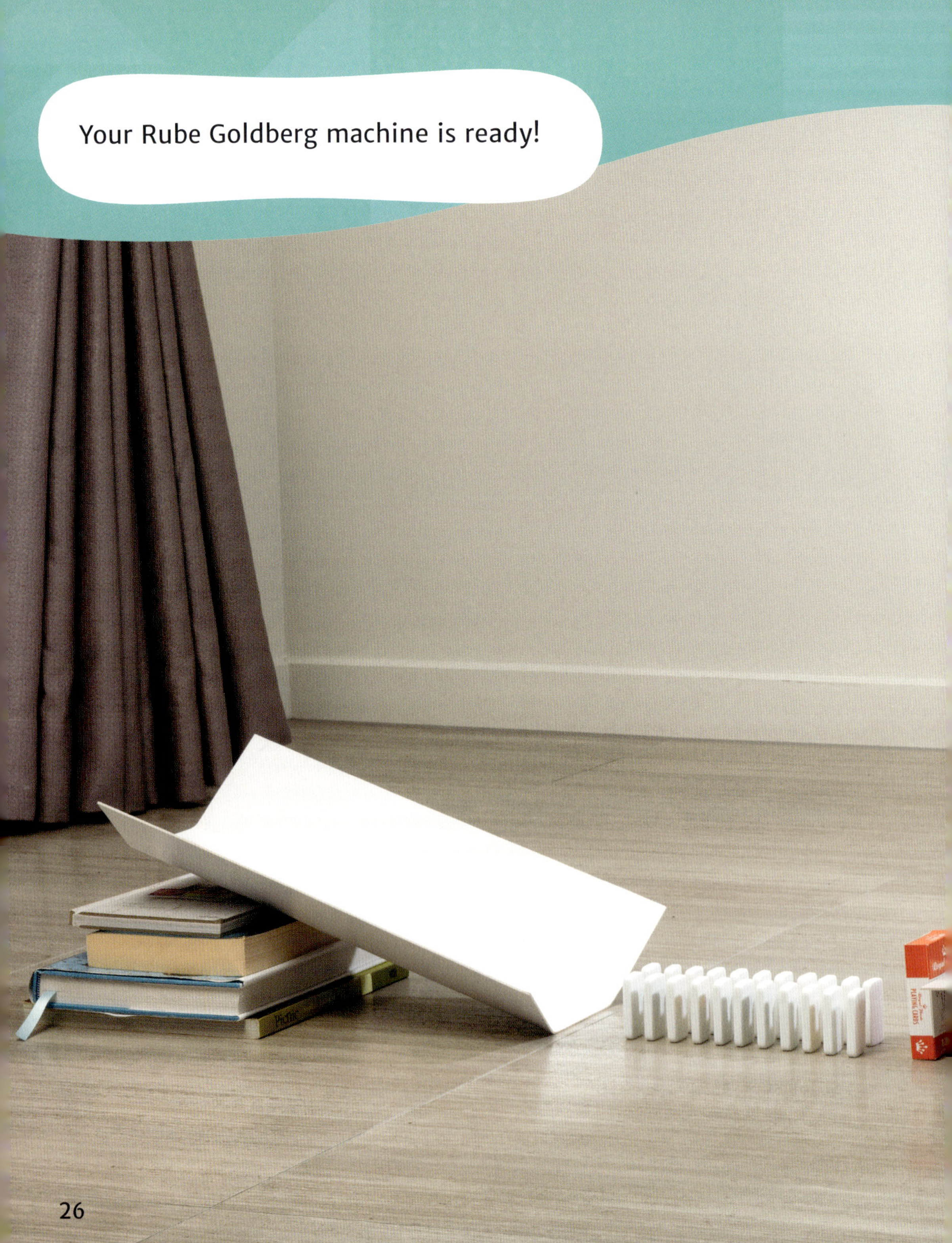

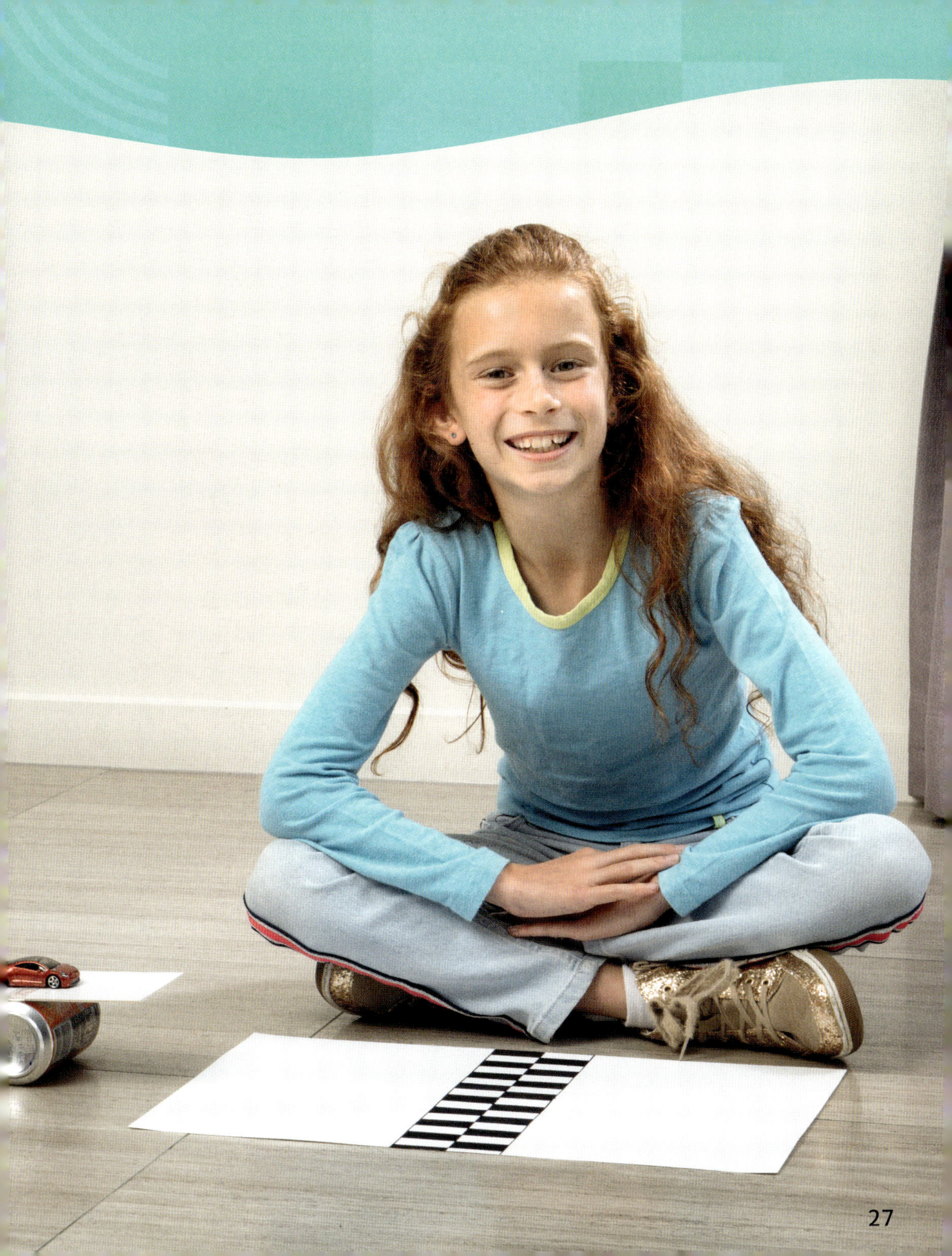

Start Your Chain Reaction

1. Take the ball and place it at the top of the ramp, then release it!
2. Watch what happens.

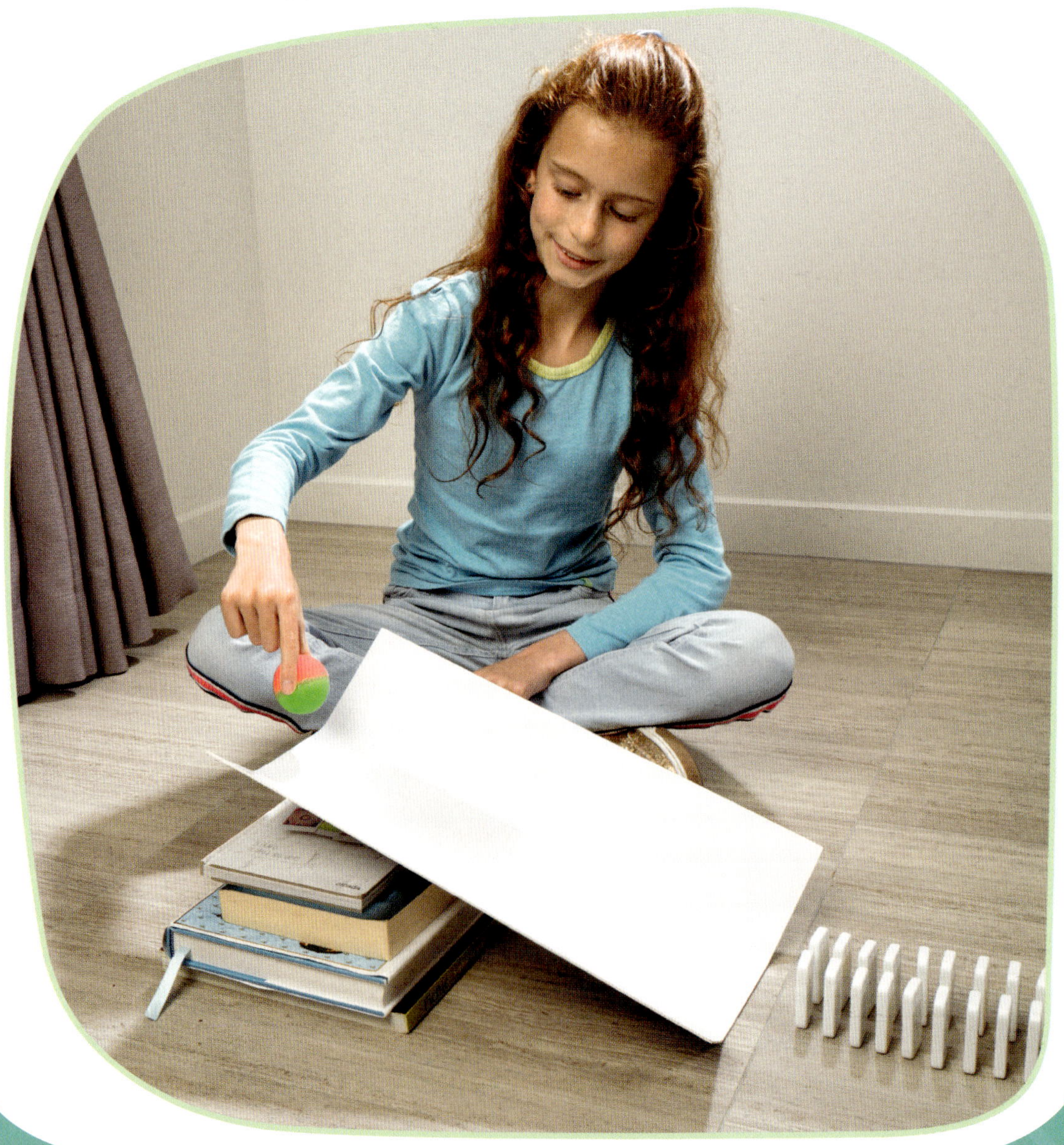

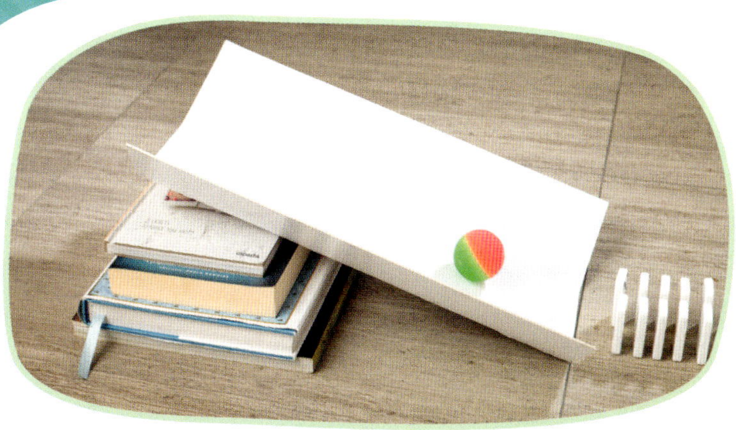

The ball rolls down the ramp and strikes the dominoes.

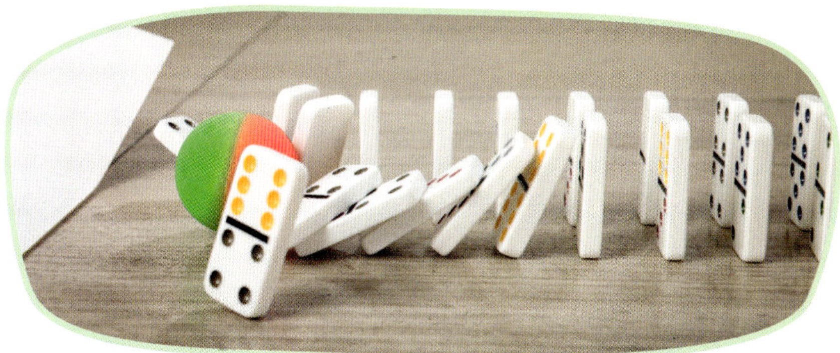

The dominoes knock each other down, one by one.

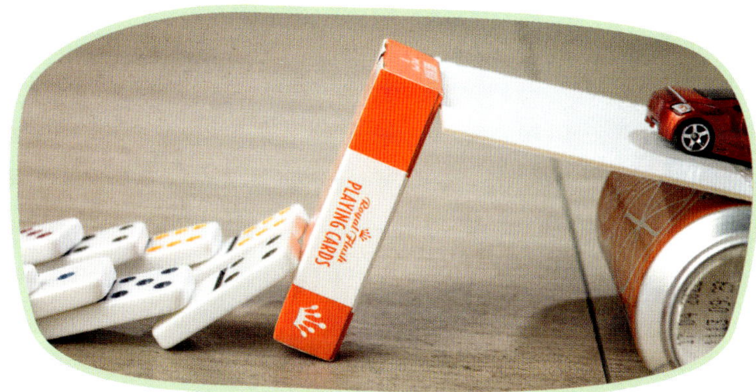

The last two dominoes knock over the pack of cards.

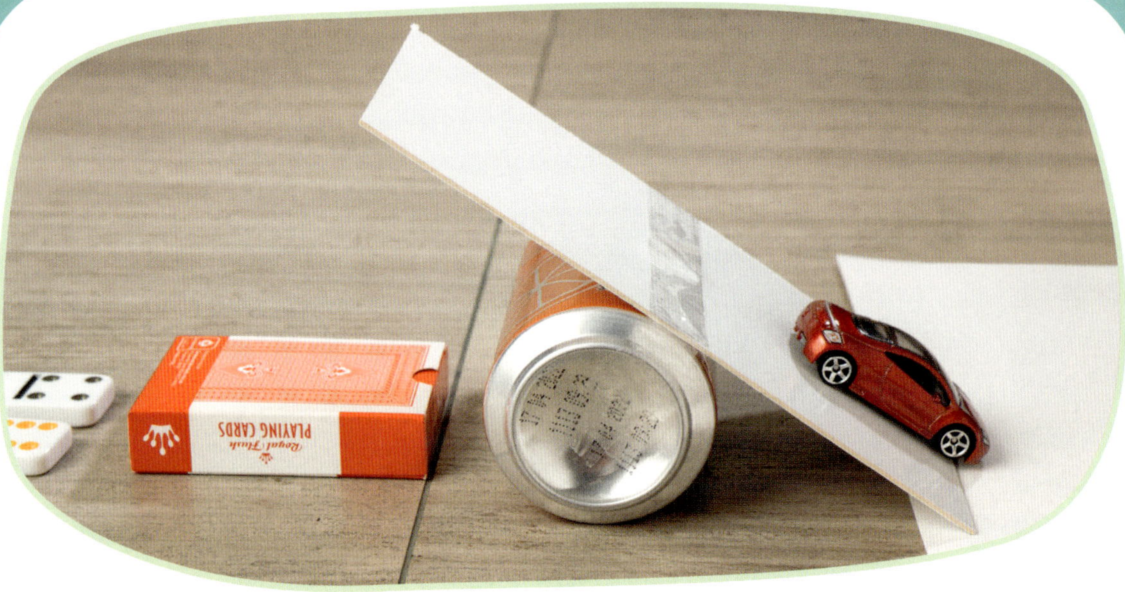

The pack of cards pushes the cardboard and makes the can turn, which makes the cardboard tilt.

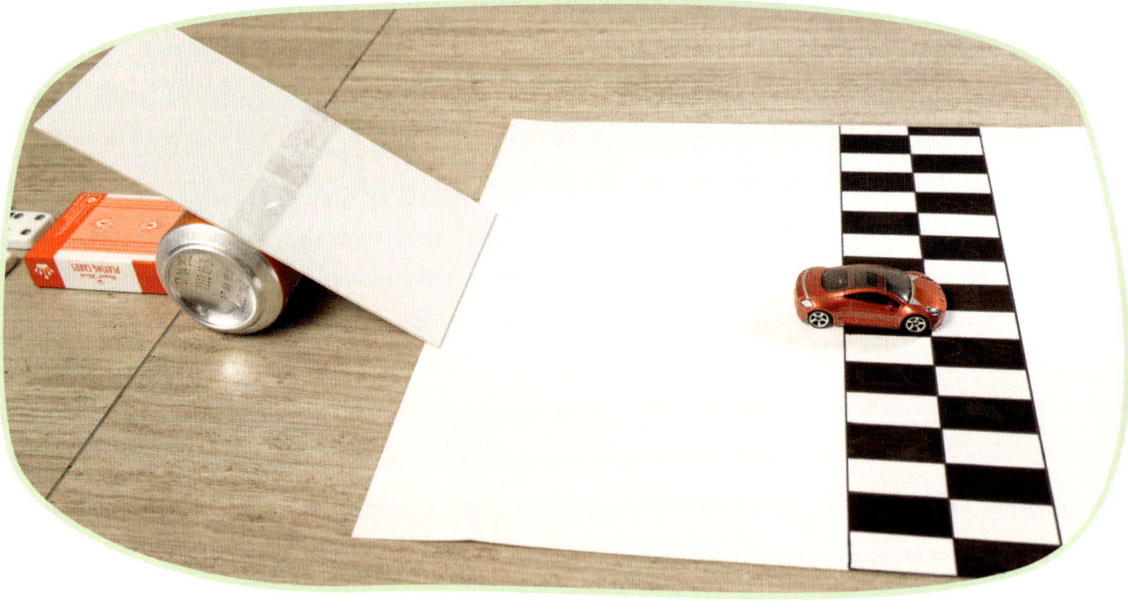

The car rolls down to the finish line.

Explaining the Science

This model uses simple machines — a ramp, a lever, and a wheel and axle — to transfer energy in a chain reaction. When the ball is released down the ramp, it has energy. This energy is then transferred to the dominoes. When each pair of dominoes falls, they too have energy, which is transferred to the next pair of dominoes. When the last dominoes hit the pack of cards, the energy is transferred to the pack of cards. The pack of cards transfers the energy to the lever (the can and cardboard) and moves the toy car (through its wheels and axles) over the finish line!

Transfer of Energy

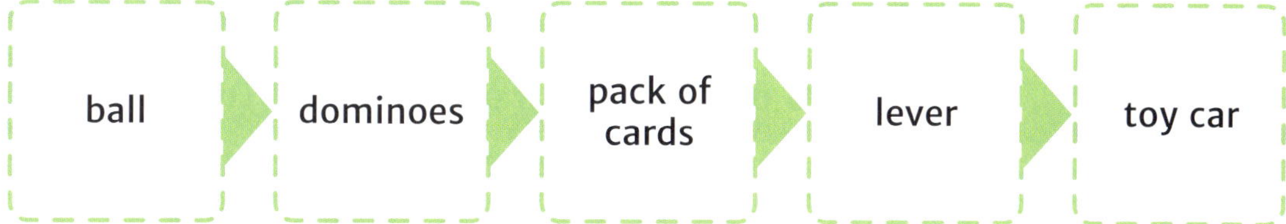

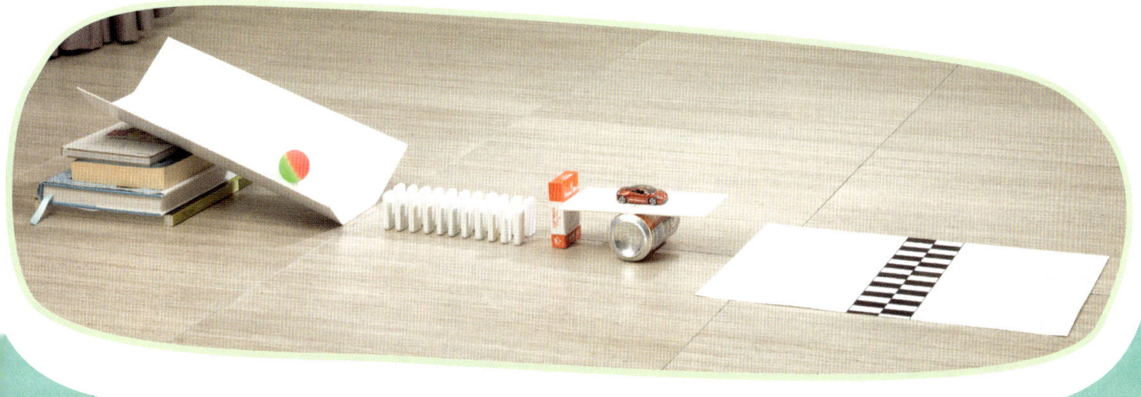

Glossary

baking soda (*noun*)	a white powder used in cooking, also called sodium bicarbonate
carbon dioxide (*noun*)	a common kind of gas
chain reaction (*noun*)	a series of events, where each event causes the next one
dab (*verb*)	to press lightly several times
energy (*noun*)	the power that makes things move
engineer (*noun*)	someone who makes machines or structures
lava (*noun*)	hot melted rock that has erupted from a volcano
lever (*noun*)	a straight bar fixed to something that can turn
magma (*noun*)	hot melted rock under Earth's surface
ramp (*noun*)	a flat sloping surface
transferred (*verb*)	moved from one place to another
wheel and axle (*noun*)	a disc (the wheel) with a rod (the axle) through the centre of it

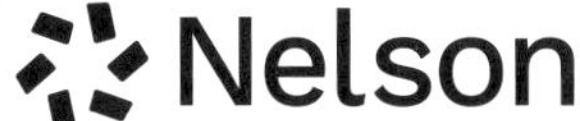

Using Science to Make Art

Text: John Burdess and Jonathon Phillips
Publisher: Eliza Webb
Editor: Jarrah Moore
Project designer: Linda Davidson
Designer: MAPG
Diagram: Fabian Slongo
Permissions researcher: Liz McShane
Production controller: Karen Young

Acknowledgements
All photographs by Lindsay Edwards Photography © 2023 Cengage Learning Australia Pty Limited, except those listed below.

We would like to thank the following for permission to reproduce copyright material:

p. 2: Alamy Stock Photo/Science Photo Library; p. 3: Shutterstock.com/SuperPuay; p. 4: Shutterstock.com/feygraphy; pp. 18, 19: Getty Images/Jeffrey Coolidge; back cover (background pattern): Shutterstock.com/sahua d.

Every effort has been made to trace and acknowledge copyright. However, if any infringement has occurred, the publishers tender their apologies and invite the copyright holders to contact them.

PM Guided Reading
Emerald Level 25

Flash Flood!
Katy and Jamini Make It Rain
On the Trail of the Playground Thief
Who's at the Zoo?
A Baby Lamb Is Too Much Trouble
Amazing Animals of South East Asia
All About Mars
Athletics
Using Science to Make Art
Far from the City

ISBN 978 0 17 033227 9

Cengage Learning Australia
Level 7, 80 Dorcas Street
South Melbourne, Victoria Australia 3205
Phone: 1300 790 853
Email: aust.nelsonprimary@cengage.com

For learning solutions, visit **cengage.com.au**

Printed in Singapore by C.O.S. Printers Pte Ltd
1 2 3 4 5 6 7 26 25 24 23 22

PM

1
2
3
4
5
6
7
8
9
10
11
12
13
14
15
16
17
18
19
20
21
22
23
24
25
26
27
28
29
30

Science can be used to make wonderful art, and art can be used to help people understand interesting scientific processes. In this book, learn how to use science to make two exciting works of art: an exploding volcano and a Rube Goldberg machine that pushes a toy car over a finish line.

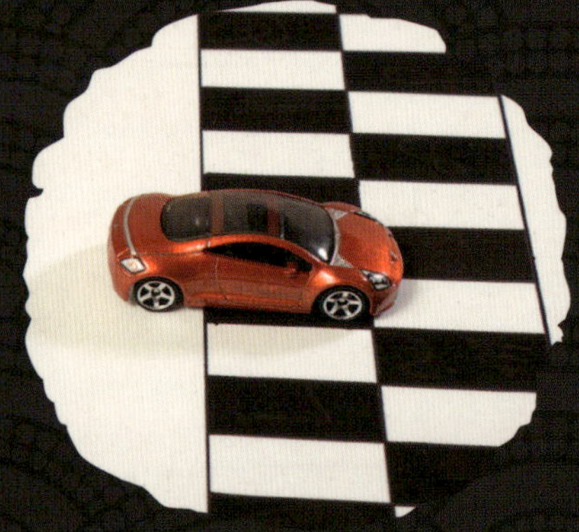

Procedure

ISBN 978-0170332279

Lev
2

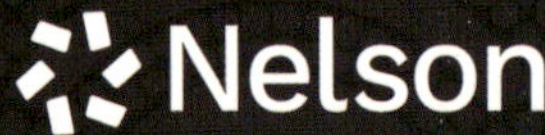